The History of BASEBALL

Diana Star Helmer and Thomas S. Owens

Rosen Classroom Books & Materials™
New York

CITY OF CHICAGO
ILLINOIS

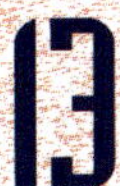

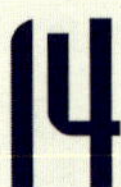

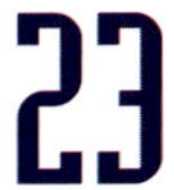

14
45
97

The History of BASEBALL

Diana Star Helmer and Thomas S. Owens

Rosen Classroom Books & Materials™
New York

Published in 2006 by The Rosen Publishing Group, Inc.
29 East 21st Street, New York, NY 10010

First Edition

Book Design: Michael de Guzman

Photo Credits: Cover (all) © Rob Tringali Jr./Sportschrome CORBIS-Bettmann; pp. 4–5, 8, 10–11, 18–19 © AP Wideworld Photos; pp. 6–7 © CORBIS-Bettmann; p. 12 © UPI/CORBIS-Bettmann; p. 15 © AP Wideworld Photos and CORBIS-Bettmann; p. 16 © Agence France Presse/CORBIS-Bettmann; p. 20 (Ruth, Sosa, McGwire) © Rob Tringali Jr./Sports Chrome USA and CORBIS-Bettmann; p. 20 (Bonds) © Reuters/Corbis.

Helmer, Diana Star, 1962-
The history of baseball / by Diana Star Helmer and Thomas S. Owens.
p. cm.—(Sports throughout history)
Includes index.
Summary: Provides an introduction to some of the key events in the development of the game that has become known as America's national pastime.
ISBN 1-4042-5540-0
1. Baseball—United States—History—Juvenile literature. [1. Baseball—History.] I. Owens, Tom, 1960- . II. Title. III. Series: Helmer, Diana Star, 1962- Sports throughout history.
GV867.5.H45 1999
796.357'0973—dc21 99-12139
CIP
AC

Manufactured in the United States of America

CPSIA Compliance Information: Batch #WR904011RC:
For Further Information contact Rosen Publishing, New York, New York at 1-800-237-9932

Contents

Around the Bases

Settlers coming to America in the early 1700s brought with them an old game called rounders that they had played in England. Rounders was played with a bat, a ball, and bases. The rules were different in different places. In later years, rounders changed into the game we now call baseball.

By 1866, when this picture of the New York Metropolitan Baseball Club was made, baseball had become more popular than rounders.

Baseball Is Born

Changes in rules slowly turned rounders into baseball. In rounders, a ball was thrown at a player to get them out. In 1845, a rounders player named Alexander J. Cartwright said that players should tag each other with the ball.

In 1858, the National Association of Baseball Players was formed. By 1860, rounders had lost its popularity in the United States. Baseball had taken its place.

Cartwright was a member of the New York Knickerbockers.

It Takes Two

The first **professional** baseball team formed in 1869. Others followed soon after. The teams joined **leagues**. The National League started in 1876. In 1900, the American League began. Since 1903, the two best teams—one from each **major league**—have played in a **championship** called the World Series.

The Cincinnati Red Stockings were the first players who were paid for full-time work.

Minor Leagues, Major Hopes

Since 1903, **minor league** teams have been a training ground for the major leagues. Each major league team has its own minor league team. Major league teams send **scouts** to **amateur** games.

If a scout finds good players there, the team hires them. These beginners play on the minor league team until they are good enough to play on the major league team.

Players often spend years in the minor leagues before they make it to the majors. Some never play for a major league team.

CITY OF CHICAGO
ILLINOIS

Women Play Ball

In 1943, the owner of the Chicago Cubs, Philip Wrigley, started the All-American Girls Baseball League (AAGBL). The women's games were popular during World War II, when men were away fighting. After the war ended and the men came back, people thought women should be at home, not on the field. The last game of the AAGBL was played in 1954.

Teams like the Chicago Colleens played softball at first. Later they played hardball, like the men.

All Together Now

At first, major league teams only let whites play. A man named Branch Rickey knew that this was wrong. He hired African American Jackie Robinson to play for the Brooklyn Dodgers. At his first game in 1947, white fans cursed and threw things at Robinson. He continued to play baseball and did not fight back.

Jackie Robinson played so well that other teams began hiring black players, too. Today, Robinson is a hero to people everywhere.

MARLINS
14
45
MARLINS
97

Baseball Grows

Early major league teams played in big cities because that's where the fans were. In the 1920s, radios allowed people all over the country to listen to games. Even more people became fans when televisions grew popular in the 1950s. The major leagues added ten teams between 1961 and 1977, and four more in the 1990s.

The Florida Marlins were one of the four teams added in the 1990s. Here the team celebrates winning its first World Series in 1997.

Strike!

In 1994, major league players went on **strike** for more pay. This meant that they wouldn't play ball until they were paid more money. There was no World Series that year.

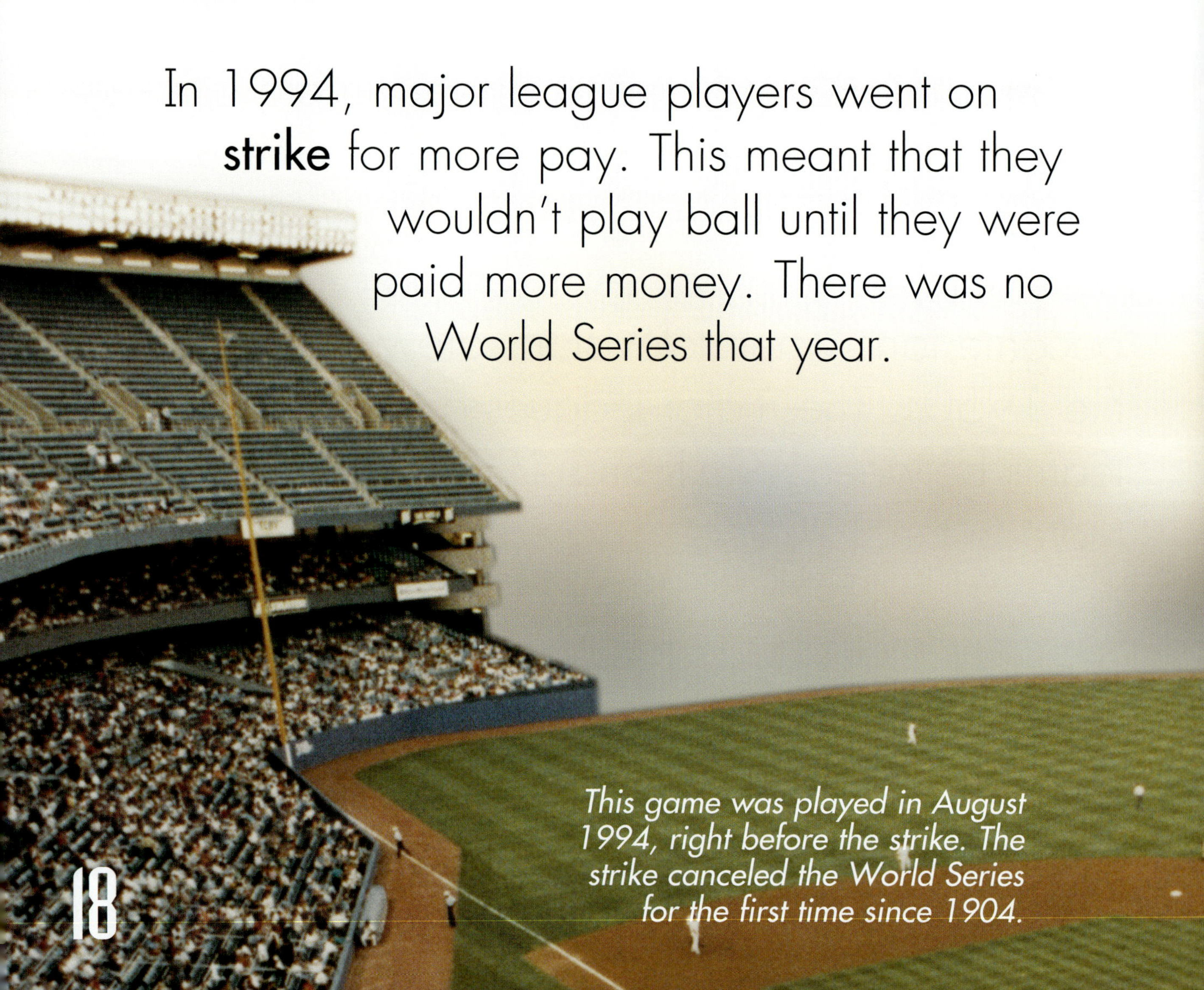

This game was played in August 1994, right before the strike. The strike canceled the World Series for the first time since 1904.

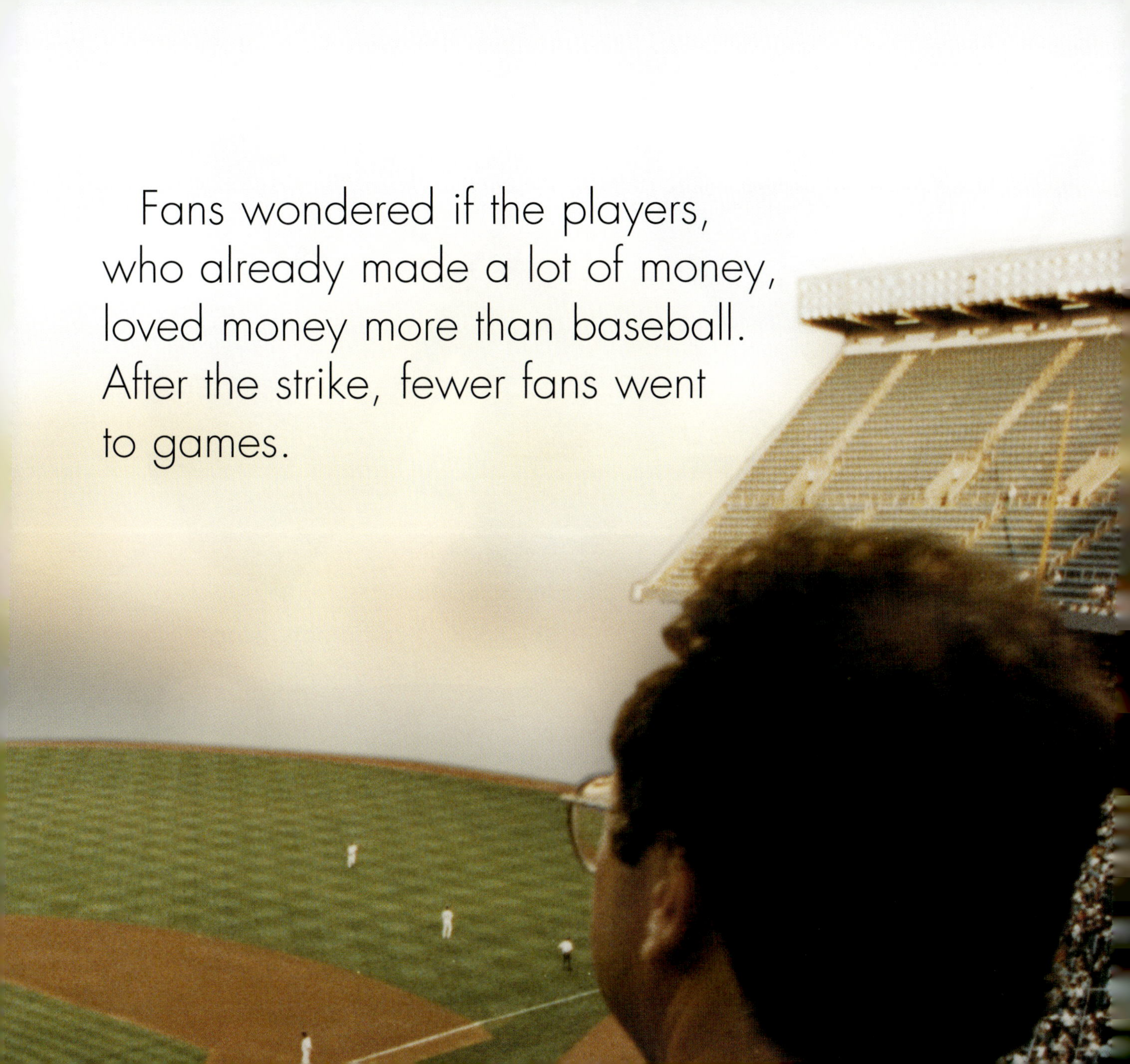

Fans wondered if the players, who already made a lot of money, loved money more than baseball. After the strike, fewer fans went to games.

Babe Ruth
Barry Bonds
Sammy Sosa
Mark McGwire

Different Ways to Win

Baseball **records** often stand unbroken for many years. In 1927, Babe Ruth hit sixty home runs in one season. No player hit more until 1961, when Roger Maris hit sixty-one. That record held until 1998, when Chicago Cub Sammy Sosa hit sixty-six and St. Louis Cardinal Mark McGwire hit seventy. In 2001, San Francisco Giant Barry Bonds set a new record with seventy-three home runs.

Babe Ruth, Mark McGwire, Sammy Sosa, and Barry Bonds are all baseball heroes.

It's a Small World

People don't just love watching baseball. They also love playing it. In 1939, a man named Carl E. Stotz started a baseball league for boys called Little League. Later, girls also played Little League baseball. Today, millions of boys and girls all around the world have fun playing baseball.

Glossary

amateur (AA-muh-chur) Someone who does something as a hobby but not a job.

championship (CHAM-pea-uhn-ship) A contest held to decide who is the best in a sport or activity.

league (LEEG) A group of teams that play against each other in the same sport.

major league (MAY-juhr LEEG) A group of the best teams in professional baseball that play against one another.

minor league (MY-nuhr LEEG) A group of professional teams that is one step below the major league.

professional (pruh-FEH-shuh-nuhl) Made up of people who are paid to play.

record (REH-kurd) The best or most that has been done.

scout (SKOWT) Someone who is paid to find talented baseball players.

strike (STRYK) An organized act by workers or players of stopping work when there are disagreements about working conditions.

Index

Web Sites

Due to the changing nature of Internet links, the Rosen Publishing Group, Inc., has developed an online list of Web sites related to the subject of this book. This site is updated regularly. Please use this link to access the list: **http://www.rcbmlinks.com/tsirc/baseball/**